Diary of an
Angry Alex: Book 5

By **Crafty Nichole**

Contents

Contents

Day Sixty-Four

4:30am

You'd think that being an actual super villain, and probably the spawn of Satan, would make Herobrine quiet and scary. Well, that might be true while he's awake, but he snores. Loud. It's unbearable. If I wasn't too scared to sleep, he'd be keeping me awake. I think Steve is still awake too. That's how loud the snoring is. If I wasn't sure he'd kill me, I'd tell him to fall in a hole. Even if he is asleep I think he could still hear me and wouldn't think it was funny.

5:00am

I wonder if Herobrine practices his evil snoring like I practice my evil laugh. I wonder if he would teach me how to do a better laugh. Maybe living with an evil genius won't be such a bad thing. He could help out with the chores, and maybe then we can all spend more time in the mines. I'll try being optimistic like that idiot Steve, and maybe things won't be so bad.

10:30am

I'm the idiot. It is so bad. Of course it's bad. Herobrine is actually evil. The face of evil, with scary glowing eyes. When he saw I was already awake, he demanded breakfast. When I told him that he burned our farm, so there wasn't any spare food, he punched me out the door, all the way to the field! I tried to go back inside and get Steve, but Herobrine set the floor on fire in front of me! Apparently, he's just that hungry. I've been farming ever since then and keeping quiet. The only good news is that the lava moat is nice hard obsidian after Steve and I dumped all of our water on it. It makes a nice, blast-proof circle in the ground. Just try blowing that up, creepers!

1:00pm

It took a long time to get the fields replanted and all of the animals fed, and wow was Herobrine in a bad mood when I got inside. He grumbled and it sounded an awful lot like a fire roaring to life. Is this guy made out of fire? Is that what makes his eyes glow?

1:20pm

It looks like there's only enough food to make everyone some bread. There won't be meat until the animals breed some more. It will have to be enough for now.

1:44pm

It's going to take a lot of adjusting to this whole "new roommate" situation. Steve finally came out of his room with the smell of baking bread. He looked as tired as I feel. Of course, he's even more scared of Herobrine than I am. But I gave Herobrine his bread, and the guy threw it back at me! Said he wanted meat! Of course we don't have any meat. Our animals are still recovering from the fires and haven't been eating well. Because of the fires. The fires that he started. Your fires, Herobrine! Fall in a hole! Okay, I didn't say any of that. I got scared and told him I'd go find more meat. We have a few spare pigs that will have to do. I can always breed more of them.

4:30pm

Steve and I might be scarred for life. The pig meat was apparently so delicious that Herobrine went out to the fields and slaughtered all the rest of the pigs! And then he threw the raw meat in my face and told me to cook it! Joke's on him. I made Steve cook it instead. Enjoy your leathery, overcooked pork chops with no cookies, you evil jerk!

4:32pm

He didn't enjoy it. He killed us both. We respawned inside the house, and then he killed us again. And he killed Steve one more time for good measure. I guess that's the way things are going to go from now on. And now I'm still exhausted and my entire body is sore.

6:00pm

So, Herobrine went out to do some mining. I'm not sure where he's going, since Steve and I blew up his old mine. No, not his mine. It was ours! We blew up our old mine! Well, I guess it doesn't matter so much where he is, just as long as he isn't here. Steve and I are busy hitting our faces against our pillows, trying to get in a short nap at least.

6:01pm

You can only sleep at night.

6:02pm

You can only sleep at night.

6:03pm

You can only—I know, I know. It's pointless to try, but I'm just so tired…

8:30pm

Just when I finally got to sleep, Herobrine barged back inside, demanding dinner. How much does this guy eat? I hope he at least brought some supplies back from the mines.

8:40pm

Nope. No supplies. He probably found a whole bunch of valuables and then destroyed them. Villain. Jerk. Monster. Yes, Herobrine is more than just a villain. He's an actual monster. And a worse one than anything I've ever dealt with before.

9:00pm

He killed all the chickens this time. I'll do the cooking and keep some hidden away to give him for breakfast. That should be good enough for now.

11:38pm

This snoring is going to drive me crazy, I just know it! How am I supposed to sleep? Is that it? Am I supposed to not sleep and then go crazy? Not this time, Herobrine! I'm too smart for your tricks!

Day Sixty-Five

2:42am

Maybe I'm not too smart for his tricks. I'm so tired I
could cry.

4:15am

I just realized…If Herobrine is a monster…and Steve
and I are supposed to kill monsters…we have to kill
Herobrine. Sure, we already tried that, but we just
have to try again. We have to try harder. We need to
kill him like we mean it. The last time we tried was a
fluke. And the time before that. And before that too.
But this time, we'll be ready. We'll make a better plan.
We'll find a way, after I manage to get some sleep.

9:00am

I was right about the snoring last night. Steve hasn't
slept either. We're both too tired to make any evil
plans right now. No, they aren't evil plans anymore.
Herobrine isn't a person, he's a monster. That makes
us heroic monster hunters! I told Steve and he laughed
for a long time, and then I started laughing too. I think

that's because we're so tired. Then, we got scared that we would wake up Herobrine, and we both went out to get a head start on the farm chores. Without any chickens or pigs, it didn't take very long. Today will be the day that we go look for more animals and start our heroic monster-slaying plans. Oh, and we ate the chicken that I was saving for Herobrine. Looks like that monster is just going to have to find his own breakfast.

4:30pm

I fail at life. Of course he found his own breakfast. Now the cows are gone too. I can't even blame Steve. It was my idea to eat the rest of the chicken. We found plenty of pigs for us to eat tomorrow, though. It looks like Herobrine only likes meat, so Steve and I can eat the garden vegetables instead. I've always wondered what it would be like to be a vegetarian. And I can eat all the cookies I want! But all of our pig herding meant that we didn't have time to talk about a plan. So far, the plan seems to be "Stuff Herobrine full of food so he doesn't burn down our house."

5:00pm

Herobrine doesn't just eat meat. He loves cookies. He just ate two stacks of cookies. I'm beginning to think that his stomach is a black hole or a bottomless pit. I wonder if he could eat Steve. At least then I wouldn't have to listen to him whine about how tired he is. I'm more tired than you are, Steve, so whine about something else!

8:00pm

Herobrine went out to do some night mining, so now there is nothing else more important than getting some sleep. I cooked up some pork chops and left them for Herobrine to eat when he gets back. Hopefully, he'll eat them and not kill our brand new pigs.

Day Sixty-Six

8:00am

It looks like I was tired enough to sleep through Herobrine's return. He's outside right now, probably looking for things to set on fire. He really does like fire, this guy. No, not a guy, he's a monster. But at least he's not a huge scaredy-cat like Steve. Steve left me a note this morning that said he was going out to look for a new place to mine, away from Herobrine.

9:00am

Way to fail at life, Alex. Herobrine just found Steve's note and ran out of the house with a diamond sword in his hand. My diamond sword, I should add. Steve's going to be really mad at me. Why didn't I get rid of the note? I really do fail at life.

9:15am

Steve just respawned at the house. I think he might cry.

9:17am

He's crying.

10:00am

Well, at least Steve isn't mad at me. After consoling him like a good friend, I told him that we need to find a good way to kill Herobrine. Not with explosives, or drowning, or crushing him in a pit of donkeys, but something that would work and keep him away for good. Steve agrees with me. I guess he's completely done trying to talk things out with Herobrine. It's for the best. You can't talk reason with a monster anyway. Believe me, I've tried.

11:00am

Steve had an idea that didn't suck. He says that we should ask the villagers about how to kill monsters. They get attacked all the time and probably know the best ways to get rid of them. The only thing is that one of us will have to keep Herobrine busy while the other one hikes up to the village. Plus, we don't have a lot to trade. It's going to look suspicious.

4:00pm

Things are going according to plan. Steve should still be on his way to the village, and I'm following Herobrine out to his mining area. He doesn't know I'm following him. If it's going to look suspicious no matter what, I'll just be super suspicious. If he notices me, he'll be more concerned with what I'm doing than what Steve is doing.

4:16pm

He noticed me. It's all going according to plan.

8:00pm

He killed me. That was definitely not a part of the plan. It took a lot of effort to find this diary and the rest of my equipment. I'll have to remember to leave it somewhere if I'm going to be anywhere near that violent monster. I just hope Steve is doing okay on his mission. I have to go to sleep now. Looking suspicious didn't help as much as I thought it would, so maybe getting a good amount of sleep will help me make a better plan tomorrow.

Day Sixty-Seven

7:30am

Steve made it back safe during the night. I want to ask him about what he learned, but Herobrine is still here in the house. We'll have to wait for him to leave before any heroic plans can be discussed.

9:00am

Just leave already.

11:00am

Leave!!

3:00pm

Steve and I have managed to do all the farm work, round up replacement animals for all the livestock that Herobrine has killed, and make enough food for three days, even with Herobrine's appetite. But Herobrine still won't just go somewhere else. Die in a fire, Herobrine! Fall in a hole and die in a fire!

3:15pm

Herobrine has just been staring at me since that last entry. Maybe the glowing eyes mean that he can see inside my head. On the off chance that he can actually read my thoughts, I'd like to just say that I'm sorry and I didn't mean it.

4:30pm

I'm not sorry. I meant every word. He was watching me because he was waiting for me to leave the room. He found my secret chest of cookies and ate all of them. Every last crumb. There isn't a hole deep enough for all of his evil. I hate him so much.

8:00pm

I finally got a chance to talk to Steve while Herobrine was out terrorizing the sheep. The villagers didn't know anything about fighting monsters. Of course they didn't. I should have known, since they get killed so easily. But they did know about some kind of underground bunker somewhere that could have secret research about monsters and stuff. But it's apparently super dangerous.

Steve and I will have to make new equipment. It shouldn't be too hard to make another mine, spend days and days mining for diamonds, smelt up some ore, craft full sets of armor, spend more days looking for a secret stronghold, and find the secret to killing Herobrine once and for all. At the same time, we'll have to keep the farm going, keep Herobrine distracted, and make sure that he doesn't figure out what we're up to.

Okay, fine. The plan needs some work. I'm still too tired to do much heroic planning. It will have to wait until morning.

8:02pm
You cannot sleep when there are monsters nearby.

8:03pm
Uh oh.

Day Sixty-Eight

4:00am

Well, Herobrine wasn't just terrorizing sheep. He lured a whole bunch of monsters into the farm. There are new creeper craters to fill in and the sheep are either dead or they all wandered off somewhere. Note to self: even if the obsidian doesn't explode, fences still do. Note to Herobrine: fall in a hole.

At least this explains what he's been up to when he leaves the house. He must have been gathering all the creepers together. There's no other way that so many of them could have found us here.

8:30am

I woke up to find Herobrine staring at me. Talk about scary! I hate his glowing eyes and his smug face. How is he so evil? Why won't he just die? Why does he want to stay here with us?

11:00am

I asked Steve the same questions, and he didn't have an answer. Let me rephrase. He does have an answer, but he didn't tell me what it is. I don't understand this whole evil twin thing, but Steve has been really weird about it. He says that Herobrine just hates him, but there's gotta be more to the story than that. Herobrine is a monster and that's a good enough reason for me to kill him. I think that Steve has his own reasons. Well, whatever. As long as he helps me slay the monster, I don't care.

1:00pm

I care. I care a lot. I have to know. Just tell me already! God, I hate Steve!

4:00pm

Nothing bad happened today. Herobrine is eating his food and keeping quiet. I'm nervous. He must be planning something. I didn't get to make any plans with Steve today either. Everything feels suspicious. There's too much secret planning going on. I'm too nervous to eat.

9:00pm

Herobrine left the house as soon as I got in bed. It's the perfect time to make a plan with Steve.

9:45pm

We have a plan. It's really simple so far:

~~Evil~~ Heroic Plan:

- Wait for Herobrine to leave

- Go the opposite direction

- Build a secret mine

- Craft good armor

- Find the secret stronghold

- Research how to kill Herobrine

- Kill Herobrine with secret stronghold knowledge

It's a place to start. It shouldn't be too hard to find someplace to make a secret mining base. It'll just be hard to keep Herobrine from knowing what we're doing.

Day Sixty-Nine

7:30am

Herobrine just left, and he went east. We'll begin our search for a good place to start mining in the west. I just woke Steve up. We'll leave after we get some food together to eat as we look.

7:45am

There's no food. Herobrine ate all of it. We have to tend to the farm before we can leave.

10:00am

The only luck we've had so far is that Herobrine hasn't come back yet. He's still doing whatever it is that he does, and there's plenty of food left for him if he gets back while we're away. I'm not sure where we'll tell him we were, but who cares. We need to get moving if we want to make any progress today.

4:30pm

We have our mine. It isn't much at the moment: a bit of coal, iron, and some granite. Nothing impressive yet, but our pickaxes broke before we could make it very deep. Steve made a whole chest full of stone ones though, so tomorrow we should be able to dig deep enough to find better materials. For now, we have to go back and try not to act suspicious.

5:00pm

On the way back, Steve suggested that we try heroic laughing. I still think mine sounds way better than his. Ha HA haha mua hee-haw ha! Still too much donkey in it, though. At least mine doesn't make me sound like a BIG JERK! Take that, Steve.

9:00pm

Herobrine still isn't home yet. It looks like our plan is working so far. It will be a lot of long days of sneaking around and mining when we can. Best get some sleep before the monster gets back.

Day Seventy

9:00am

I can't believe that Steve can still be such a jerk! Even with our new heroic plan, he still goes off on his own, leaving me to do the farm work! He left a note saying that he wanted to get some mining done and that I should "take care of things at home." He's just lucky I found it before Herobrine this time. I'm so angry that I punched a sheep to death on accident instead of shearing it. Looks like we'll be having mutton for lunch just the monster and me.

12:00pm

Herobrine might not be a monster after all. He brought a whole herd of sheep back from...wherever it is that he goes. Steve still isn't back. Herobrine hasn't said anything about it, but he has to have noticed that Steve's missing. I don't care much about what happens to Steve right now, but I won't let this ruin my heroic plans!

1:00pm

Steve still isn't back. I should add a secret mission into the plan. A mission where I can also kill Steve.

3:25pm

Herobrine left again, so I started practicing my heroic laugh. Steve is going to be so jealous when he gets back. It'll be fantastic, wonderful, magnificent, and 100% donkey-free!

3:45pm

So, it isn't really donkey-ish anymore. I did notice a few rabbits watching me through the window though. Weird. Maybe I'll bake some cookies instead of all this laughing. I need to refill my secret stash anyway.

4:00pm

I had to go to the jungle area to get cocoa for the cookies. It wasn't a long journey; one of the donkeys gave me a ride. But guess who I found once we got to the jungle—Herobrine. He was burning down the whole jungle! With lava! He was just pouring buckets and buckets of lava off of one of the tall trees. Where does he keep finding so much freaking lava? He must have found Steve's old nether portal. All I know is that I managed to rescue some cocoa and some jungle saplings, but I'll have to find a secret place to replant them. No cookies for anyone today. Time to go back home I guess.

5:30pm

That Steve really knows how to make me mad. He was at the house when I got back, and he has the nerve to lecture me about making him wait for me. That guy, ugh, I hate him. He's just lucky that we have to work together to take care of our monster problem.

Anyway, Steve had good news from the mine. He struck diamonds! Not that I'll get to see any of them. He left them behind in a chest. I hope they'll still be there next time we get a chance to mine. Steve also said that the only reason he came back was because he ran out of food. We need to find a way to keep Herobrine from eating EVERYTHING we bring in from the farms, without making it so that he kills all of our animals. I don't know if those sheep were a one-time thing, but maybe if Herobrine keeps bringing in new livestock, it won't matter so much if he eats some of them from time to time.

Steve says he left a furnace in the mine, and that it's smelting up some iron. There will be enough for two full suits of armor, and Steve thinks that after we craft those, it will be time to set out looking for this stronghold. I think we should wait a bit, maybe enchant our armor. Iron isn't super durable on its own. But then Steve pointed out that we don't have a lot of time before Herobrine notices that we're up to something, if he hasn't already. And even if we did have the time, neither of us could hold on to our experience levels for very long with Herobrine constantly murdering us. I guess it's all true. I hate it when Steve gets reasonable. It makes it hard to disagree with him, and I hate agreeing with him.

But, it's time to move on to the next part of the plan: locate the secret stronghold. We'll have to start back at the village and get better directions. Apparently when Steve asked where the stronghold is, the villagers just said "underground."

To mark the end of a successful planning session, Steve and I shared a heroic laugh. I don't feel like killing him anymore. Sure, I'd still like him to fall in a hole and I'll always want to punch him a little, but I don't think I want him dead. Hmm. I guess I'm starting to feel more like a hero!

7:00pm

With how much Herobrine eats, Steve and I decided to start adding in another farming shift after dinner. Herobrine ate pretty much every scrap of food in the house, except the carrots, so there's a lot to do. Steve said that he saw a flock of chickens over by the secret mine, so he went to go fetch them. At least, I hope that's what he's doing. If he gets another chance to do the mining instead of the farming, I'll take back what I said about not wanting him dead.

8:00pm

Steve came back with chickens. I guess he's off the hook. Herobrine came back with more sheep, also. I'm not sure what he's up to, but I also noticed that all of the sheep have been sheared. I thought that Steve did it, but he's been away all day. What are you planning, Herobrine?

Day Seventy-One

3:16am

Well, where to start? Herobrine can go and find the biggest, darkest, most spider-infested hole, and then he can just FALL IN IT!! He burned down our house, and then blew it up. He did shear those sheep, and he set all the wool inside and set it on fire. I didn't realize what was happening until I was already on fire. And underneath the wool, Herobrine had left us a nice layer of TNT. Why would he do that?? Why does he have to be so evil?

My bed burned to pieces and then exploded, and it was a long walk back to the crater that used to be our house. Steve's here, already starting to rebuild. I'm surprised that anything survived the fire, but the whole farm is fine. Steve and I were blown up, but the kitchen area is fine. I guess that's what Herobrine finds most important. I'm glad that this diary wasn't destroyed. Steve found it for me (I wonder if he read any of it) and said I should keep it somewhere safe. Well, Steve, nowhere is safe. Obviously.

I'm going to go and collect some supplies from the secret mine so that we can make some progress. I don't know where Herobrine is, but I hope he just stays away. I've had more than enough of his monster mischief for today, and it isn't even morning yet.

6:00am

Herobrine still hasn't shown his face. Steve and I finished rebuilding, and this house has a separate room just for Herobrine and a secret obsidian basement where we can hide some stuff. Food especially. And my diary. Pretty much everything valuable that we still try to keep in the house. Plus, I made sure that Herobrine has his own room. I'm tired of waking up to his horrible, horrible glowing eyes staring at me first thing in the morning.

Ahh, all of the diamond gear here that Herobrine hadn't already taken was burned to a crisp and then blown up. Curse you Herobrine, you fiendish monster person. I'm so glad we already have a plan to kill him. It's too early in the morning to make any new murder plans, and you CAN ONLY SLEEP AT NIGHT, YES I KNOW THAT! I'm just so tired. Getting murdered is pretty exhausting.

9:00am

Still no sign of Herobrine. I think he might be keeping his distance until we have the house fully repaired again. Joke's on him. Steve and I took care of the chores and we slaughtered all of the extra sheep that Herobrine had been bringing back, so now there's plenty of mutton. We're going to the village today. There's no reason to stick around here anymore. We won't return until we find a way to destroy Herobrine once and for all.

2:00pm

The village looks so peaceful compared to all the fire and destruction of last night. There are so many villagers wandering about, offering terrible trades and honking at each other. I even saw some children. I guess they feel safe with their iron golem looking out for them. Maybe I should make them another one. Then they'd be twice as happy. Whoa, hold up there! It's so weird having these heroic thoughts all the time! First thing's first, we have to find someone who knows anything about the stronghold.

3:00pm

The butcher and farmers don't know anything. I'm starting to get frustrated, but Steve hasn't given up yet. I just want to punch these stupid villagers. Forget making them another golem. I just want them to start being useful and to stop offering such terrible trades.

3:10pm

I really want to punch them all to death. They keep bumping into me and honking in that awful way that they do. Maybe the librarian will know more about the secret stronghold.

4:45pm

Success! The librarian did know. So did the priest that Steve talked to. They both say that the stronghold is buried deep underneath the jungle. I haven't checked on it since it was covered in lava, but maybe that's for the best. With all the lava, there won't be too many monsters in that area. As long as we're careful, we should be able to find it without any problems. We're on the way there now.

5:00pm

Well, thinking about it, the jungle is a long way from here. We'll have to go past both our secret mine and the house to get there. I hope we don't run into Herobrine. Maybe we should just stay in the mine tonight. Even wearing a full suit of armor, I don't feel very confident. The monster is just too scary.

8:30pm

We're down in the mine for the night. We don't have beds, but that's okay. We can spend all night looking for more diamonds. I have a feeling we'll need them sooner or later. At least Steve listened to me and made the diamonds we already had into an enchanting table. There was even enough to make one sword. Steve can use it since he found the diamonds, but I'm not leaving this mine until I have one of my own.

11:00pm

Still no diamonds.

Day Seventy-Two

2:20am

Still no diamonds.

4:30am

I found three diamonds! I decided to make them into a pickaxe. We're about to have a lot of digging to do, and I intend to do it in style. There's bound to be some obsidian in the way after Herobrine's lava spree. I really hope Herobrine won't come looking for us. This mine has to stay a secret.

7:00am

We'll be leaving soon. There's no point in putting it off. After a bit to eat, we're going towards the used-to-be-a-jungle. It's probably all just one big lava pit at this point.

9:30am

We passed by the house a while ago. Herobrine wasn't there. I'm starting to worry that he knows we're trying to kill him. Well, I guess it doesn't matter. He'll figure it out one way or another. We're almost to the jungle. Steve needed a break to kill some pigs. I'm not sure where they came from, but we definitely could use the extra food. We're about to spend a long time combing the jungle for any sign of a structure. It'll apparently be made out of stone bricks, so it shouldn't be hard to recognize.

10:30am

I'm going to paint you a word picture of the weirdness that Herobrine turned this jungle into. It's a nightmare to say the least. There's an ocelot on fire over there. Steve actually got sick. There's a huge amount of smoke just everywhere. The lava has settled into pools, but there's a massive pillar of lava suspended in the air. It's so bright that it probably looks exactly the same at night. There are a few trees still on fire at the very edges of the jungle. I guess it doesn't really count as a jungle anymore. It's a big fiery pit. Maybe it's supposed to be like the nether. It doesn't have quite the same feeling as the nether, but I do feel like we're being watched. It's really uncomfortable.

Like it or not, we're going to have to start digging now. It's going to be a loooong day.

4:00pm

No stronghold yet. Mostly, it's just been Steve and me dodging lava and trying to find a good place to start digging. Maybe Herobrine knew about the stronghold all along. Maybe he's there already, just waiting for us. Oh man, I hope not.

We're making a base camp for now, building it out of cobblestone so nothing catches on fire. We have beds with us and I don't expect any mobs to come for us with all of this lava, but it's still better to have a base just in case things don't quite go as planned. I can't help but notice that my plans don't always tend to go as planned.

8:00pm

The beds are set up and we already have some iron smelting from the small bit of digging we've done so far. Looks like there's nothing left to do today but get to sleep. Finally! A decent night's sleep where I don't have to worry about Herobrine's awful snoring or waking up to his terrible glowing eyes!

Day Seventy-Three

7:00am

Early start today. I'm still so worn out, but we have to keep moving forward in our heroic quest. This lava lake isn't very big, really. There should be plenty of time to search underneath all of it today. Once we find a cave system, it'll be a piece of cake. Oh, I still have that cocoa. Maybe I'll use it to bake a cake! It will really help lift our spirits!

7:15am

Wow, these noble and nice thoughts are really getting out of hand. Even though we're allies and comrades in this monster hunt, Steve is still a jerk and my frenemy. I have to keep up my guard and make sure he doesn't ruin the heroic plan.

2:00pm

I feel like we're getting close. We did find a small cave system that we're lighting up with torches. Hopefully there will be some kind of indicator that we're headed in the right direction, but I doubt it will be that easy.

The priest Steve talked to said something about crafting some kind of tool out of ender pearls, but we just do not have the time to go out hunting Endermen. We'll just have to do this the old-fashioned way and hope we get lucky.

Right now, we're taking a break to get some fresh air and eat. I'm going to leave this diary here at the base from now on. If I keep it with me, there's always the risk that I'll die some horrible way and it'll vanish before I can get back to it. So, bye for now. Hopefully I'll be back soon with good news.

???pm

My clock is lost somewhere in that horrible, horrible death trap, but it has to be some time in the afternoon. I'm back with some good and bad and worse news. The bad news is obviously that I died and lost all of my stuff, including my diamond pickaxe. We found the stronghold, is the good news.

The worse news is a little more complicated. The whole time that we were digging around underground, I kept feeling someone was watching me. At first it was pretty easy to ignore. I didn't think too much of it; there's always some kind of creepy thing hanging out in the dark caves. There have definitely been more bats down here than I'm used to seeing. But then it started to feel more and more like Herobrine was lurking somewhere, waiting for one of us to let our guard down. I got distracted and didn't even realize that I had started walking on stone brick instead of regular stone. I didn't realize until I broke one of the brick blocks and held it in my hand. I called out for Steve to come see, and he ran over. We got excited and stopped being careful.

This is where things get weird. One of the blocks that we broke had something in it. Something…alive. And angry. It was small and gray and easy enough to kill, but it kept jumping into blocks and pulling out more and more of the awful things. They overwhelmed us and killed us in a matter of moments. There's no way that we can get all the way back in time to rescue our lost items. Well, no way we could survive the trip down and the horrible horde of teeny hopping nightmares.

At any rate, the sun has started to go down and we have no real food left. I did bake a cake, but I don't expect it to last past breakfast. And if I hear one complaint out of Steve, I'm gonna punch him into the lava lake.

Day Seventy-Four

7:30am

Just as I thought, Steve complained about the cake. I only punched him once, though. He didn't get anywhere near the lava, so I don't know why he's still whining about it. He ate the cake at least. We are going to have to find some food before going back into the stronghold though.

12:00pm

After a bit of foraging, we have some food to take with us and also plenty to leave behind in the base. There isn't a lot of armor between the two of us, but we both have swords. It'll have to do for now. I'm leaving the diary behind again, so...wish me luck I guess?

12:15pm

I had a brilliant idea. Those hellish gray fuzzballs probably don't like lava so much. Probably less so if it gets poured on their heads. I'm going to use the last if our iron to craft a bucket. It's gotta work.

3:00pm

So, another good news/bad news thing happened. The good news is that I killed the silverfish (that's what Steve calls them, but it doesn't really give a good idea of how vicious the little beasts are). The bad news is that I killed Steve. Not only that, but his iron gear was destroyed too. I went back through the cave system and collected a few more chunks of ore, along with plenty of coal. Something tells me that this stronghold is going to be massive and completely dark. We'll be ready to go back down once Steve finishes crafting his replacement armor.

Day Seventy-Five

???am

I'm not sure what time of night it is. I'm assuming it's after midnight, but that's always hard to figure out during a new moon. There are a lot of things that I'm not sure about, but I know that Steve is verrry mad at me.

The lava I dumped on the silverfish flooded a part of the stronghold. One of the libraries we found was completely on fire when we got to it. Why do I fail at life? I obviously didn't mean to. Steve thinks I did it on purpose though. He accused me of working with Herobrine because of all the times I tried to kill Steve back in the day. A few weeks ago. Whenever.

There are other libraries down there though. I'm sure we'll be able to find something useful in those bookshelves. All I know for sure is that we're running out of time. There isn't much left to do but jump into that research…after Steve gets another set of armor.

He doesn't have to take it so personally though. I already apologized enough. If he doesn't believe me, then fine. But I do still need his help to kill Herobrine.

2:00pm

It's hard to explain exactly what we found down there in the dark. There were plenty of monsters and a bunch more of those silverfish things, though. We found a few more libraries, and they were all pretty useless. All of the books were moldy and falling apart. Except the ones that were on fire. Those ones were just on fire. Steve is less angry with me about that at least. The books that we could read all turned out to be some kind of cookbooks. Some of them might have been for brewing potions, but it was really hard to tell.

But the biggest discovery was this strange looking portal-type thing. Steve says it's a portal, anyway. It isn't connected or turned on or however it is that portals work, but that shouldn't be too hard to figure out…maybe? There were a few orbs lining the edges that kind of looked like eyes. Some of them were missing though. Maybe we should try to find more of those somewhere.

But Steve has this crazy theory that this portal leads to somewhere even worse than the nether. Someplace with a monster that's even worse than Herobrine. I wonder how that's even possible, but it's the best chance we have for now, so I say that we should try it.

The End…that's what Steve called it. Well, I guess that means we should ask an Enderman where to find the rest of these eyes. We're going to wait for nighttime and then head out. I'm getting really tired of Steve complaining about things though. He keeps saying, "It's too hot!" Well, of course it is. It's a lava lake, Steve. That's gonna be pretty hot. I really should punch him into it. Maybe once Herobrine is taken care of.

10:20pm

Endermen are still really scary. I forgot about the horrible sounds they make. *Shudder.* We have a few ender pearls now, and Steve thinks he knows how to make them into ender eyes. That priest must have told him how. Either that or he's just a huge liar. I can't believe he wants to drag us through the nether. He has all these terrible stories about times he almost died in there, and now he wants to make me go there? I've seen more than enough lava these days. Maybe if I ask nicely, he'll let me stay behind. Or at least let me go back to the house?

11:00pm

He isn't going to let me skip out on this one. Well, at any rate, we got to practice our heroic laughter a little bit. Not even one donkey came out this time! Progress! But there was this group of rabbits hanging around for a while afterwards. I don't get it. What noise does a rabbit even make???

Day Seventy-Six

8:00am

We slept, we've eaten, and all of our gear is packed. It's time to go to the nether. It's too dangerous to go back to Steve's first portal, especially if Herobrine already knows about it. We can make a brand new portal out here with all of the obsidian I mined from underneath the lava lake. We have exactly enough. There's no way I'm taking this diary with me to a place with even more lava. This is turning into a huge quest. Hopefully I'll be back with good news.

5:00pm

What a complete disaster! Steve needs to fall down a hole and hit his head and die. We were doing so well! We made it to a fortress and were killing blazes, doing fine, when I get withered by a black skeleton. I tried to run behind Steve to wait out the wither effect, and then Steve hit me with his sword! Right in the face!! Why do we fail so miserably? I hope he managed to escape from there with the things we need. He probably did, that jerk. Probably has my entire inventory. He hasn't respawned back here with me, so that's a good sign, right?

It's not fair. I hope he dies horribly, but that would be bad for our plans.

9:30pm

He's still not back. I'm starting to actually worry. He definitely didn't die, because if he did, he would spawn right here with me. But he hasn't come back out of the portal either. Well, I'll try sleeping and see if he turns up in the morning.

11:30pm

Terrible news. Steve just got back. When he left the nether, he used the wrong portal and he ended up back at the house. Guess who was waiting for him? Yep. Herobrine. He hasn't found this base yet, but it looks like we're going to have to go and distract him so that he doesn't figure out what we've been planning. He's apparently asleep right now, so we have a whole walk back to come up with a convincing enough lie to tell.

Day Seventy-Seven

9:00am

Oh my notch, I can't believe that worked. Steve was busy working out some complicated story about looking for pigs to ride, but I decided on a more direct approach. I told Herobrine that we were out looking for a way to get rid of him, but that we couldn't find anything. We were back because we'd given up on trying to kill him. And it worked!

Herobrine went off again, like he usually does. He did kill the very last of our animals before he left though; there was only one cow left. I think he kept it alive just so that he could kill it in front of us, actually. This guy must be super bored without us to torment. Whoa, whoa, whoa! Again with the hero thoughts! I almost felt bad for that monster! I have to be more careful about that. Even if it's a part of my heroic nature to try to find the best in people, Herobrine isn't a person.

3:40pm

It's going to take a lot of work to convince Herobrine that we're here to stay, especially since we need to start collecting supplies to enter the End. Steve and I went around collecting a few stray animals. We only found two chickens and a pig, but it's better than nothing. We'll have to keep Herobrine distracted somehow, while we keep mining out our secret mine. We lost most of our equipment in the lava, and my armor is useless now. Steve says that I can go mining first for once, probably because he feels guilty for killing me in the nether. Well, he SHOULD feel guilty! Every time I try to work with that guy he just ends up getting in my way! Not this time. I'm not coming back until I have a dozen diamonds.

9:00pm

I've struck diamond! Only four so far, but it's a good start! I'll probably be mining all night at this rate though. Luckily there were still some carrots in the farm. It's at least enough to keep me going.

Day Seventy-Eight

5:30am

I didn't find a dozen diamonds, but I do have ten. That's enough to start crafting some gear. To keep it fair, I'll make something for Steve too, even though he never makes me anything. Well, he can have a pair of boots. I'll have my own pair and a sword. That should be enough for now. Time to get back home and probably do all the farming also. *Sigh*

9:15am

Such a pleasant surprise! When I got back to the house, Steve was already almost done with the farm chores! He didn't do any cooking, but that's for the best. It was probably really uncomfortable to be alone with Herobrine. I'll find out how that feels this afternoon while Steve goes off to mine. I told him about the boots, and he was actually very pleased. I always forget that it isn't the worst thing to be nice to that guy. Even if he almost never deserves it.

Time to cook.

3:00pm

Steve left for the mine about an hour ago. Herobrine came back and was curious, but didn't ask any questions. Actually, it's been a long time since I heard him talk. That's just fine. I could go a whole lifetime without hearing that awful voice of his again.

5:30pm

Uncomfortable silence at dinner tonight. Herobrine is eating a chicken and I'm eating bread, and there's just nothing to distract me from how terribly awkward all of this is. So I'm writing in here instead. I wonder if he knows how to read.

5:35pm

Of course he knows how to read. I just offended him a lot and now he's killing the animals again. My bad, how was I supposed to know? It's not as if he ever tries to have a conversation!

9:00pm

I'm so happy we made Herobrine his own bedroom. I can hear him snoring through the wall. Steve isn't back yet. I want to go mine with him, but I'm not going to risk Herobrine following me there. Not when the plan is so close to completion! Well, I guess the plan needs a bit of reworking. Let's see.

Heroic Plan 2.0:

- Find the secret stronghold [check]

- ~~Research how to kill Herobrine~~ Finish the portal

- ~~Kill Herobrine with secret stronghold knowledge~~ Find the scary End monster

- Let the monster kill Herobrine

- Punch Steve into the lake of lava

It's all coming together. We just need to keep everything secret until we're ready to get rid of Herobrine once and for all! I'm going to do a heroic laugh as quietly as I can now.

A rabbit just hopped up to my window. That's not funny. What about this laugh sounds anything like a rabbit??

Day Seventy-Nine

8:00am

We're almost ready to meet the monster. The new monster. The big one...you know which one I mean. We're almost ready to get to the End. Steve found a LOT of diamonds and even made me a chest plate! It was a nice gesture. We can do this. We just need to gather some food, and for some reason, Steve said we might want to get some pumpkins. Pumpkins! Not even to make into pie. He wants to wear them on our heads! Well, if he really thinks it will work, I'll give it a try. He did use up his diamonds to make me armor. I'll wear a pumpkin on my head for a diamond chest plate any day.

11:00am

We're in the same kind of struggle as before, where Herobrine just won't leave for the day. GO AWAY! CAN'T YOU SEE THAT WE ARE TRYING TO KILL YOU?? It's just rude!

2:00pm

Oh! Okay! He's gone! Time to put the plan into motion! To the lava lake!

4:30pm

We have plenty of food, so we sprinted all the way here. Steve has the gear, I have pumpkins, there's nothing to stop us from getting to the monster. We can do this! Herobrine, we had a good game of cat and mouse, but now it's time for you to get dead! I'll be leaving the diary behind again, and hopefully I'll be back with a story of how Steve and I vanquished the evil monster, Herobrine!

Day Eighty

10:26am

Nothing went as planned. I don't know what day it is. I don't know any of what just happened. Everything feels so strange. I guess I should start at the beginning.

We made it safely through the stronghold to the portal room. There were a few mobs, but nothing we couldn't handle with our equipment. No silverfish, that's for sure. But once we stepped through the portal, everything went strange. The atmosphere there was so crushing. I couldn't tell if the air was thicker or if the gravity was different or if I just felt weird wearing a pumpkin on my head. It doesn't really matter. The End is such a weird place. There are Endermen roaming around all over the place. I stared at the ground, terrified of angering any of them. Steve said it was fine with the pumpkins, but I felt like being careful.

The monster wasn't hard to find. It was a dragon. A huge, black, scary dragon. It looked at me like I was nothing at all. I've never felt so small. Steve started to talk to it, but it didn't matter. The dragon attacked us. Of course it did. Everything always attacks us. And

Steve always just tries talking to the things! I should have guessed that it would happen that way.

But that isn't the worst part. The worst part is that Herobrine was there. He was in the End. He was riding the dragon. Herobrine was the most powerful monster all along. And he probably knew about our heroic plan the whole time.

Curse you, Herobrine. I hate you and your glowing eyes and your super loud snoring and your laugh made of actual evil. That was the worst part of dying this time, was hearing his awful laugh, as the dragon murdered me.

So now, we're in hiding. Steve and I are in the village now. The village I built up. The one with the villagers that sent us to multiple deaths. I hate it here. I hate it, I hate the villagers, I hate Steve, and I hate Herobrine. Mostly though, I'm scared. Herobrine riding a dragon…it's something I wish I had never seen.

For now, Steve and I are building up a small army of iron golems to try to keep ourselves safe in this village, but who knows how long that could last. Herobrine is still out there somewhere. I hope we'll be ready when he comes back for us.

To be continued...

Made in the USA
Coppell, TX
09 December 2024

42077748R00036